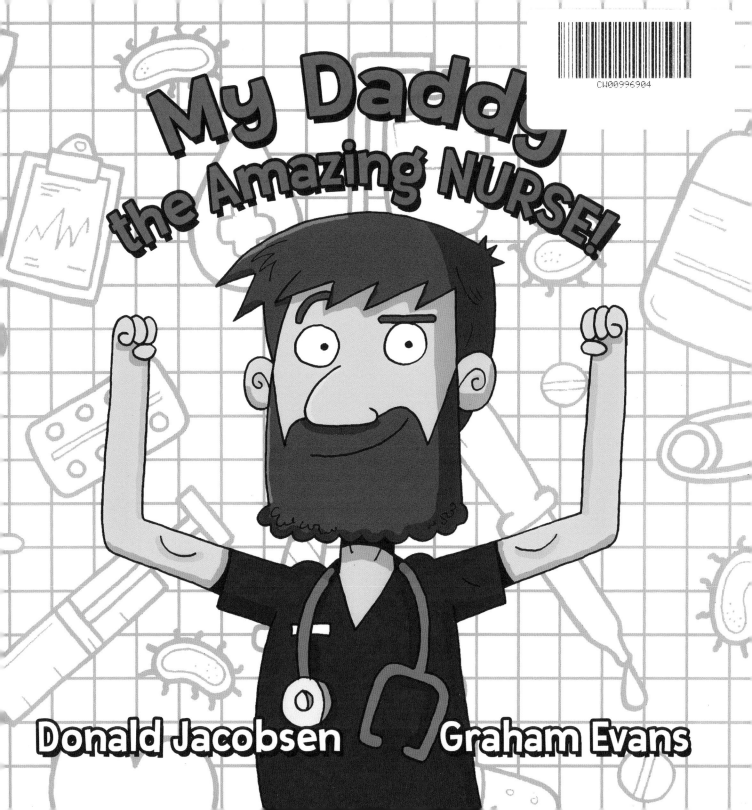

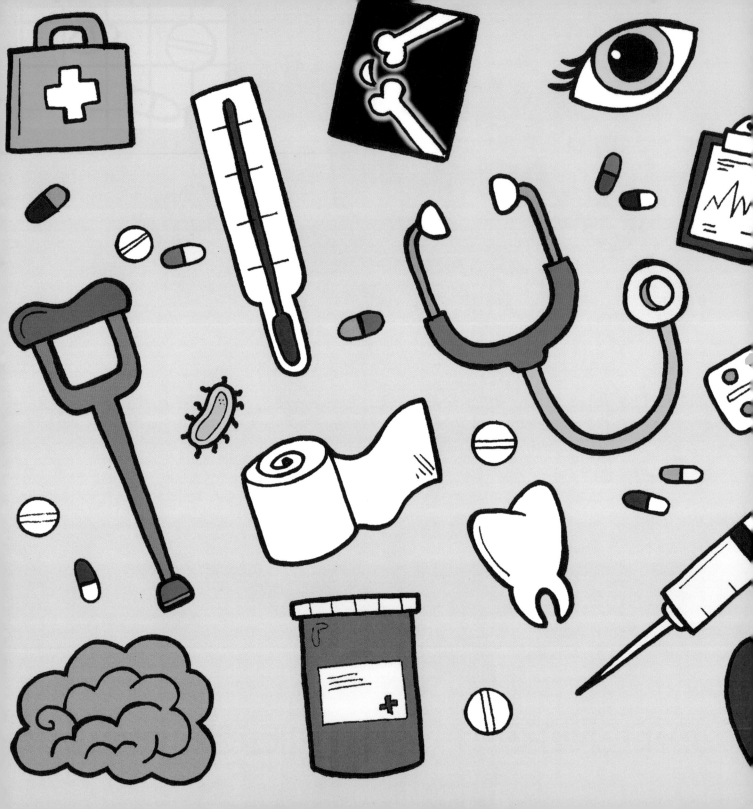

My Daddy, the Amazing Nurse
A Rhyming Career Exploration Book for Children

Big Ideas for Little Dreamers Series #3
Written by Donald Jacobsen
Illustrated by Graham Evans

Second Edition

an imprint of Three Suns Press
Memphis, Tennessee

All content copyright ©2016, 2019-2020 Donald Jacobsen. All rights reserved. Without limiting the rights under the copyright reserved above, no part of this publication may be reproduced, stored in, or introduced into a retrieval system, or transmitted in any form or by any means (electronic, mechanical, photocopying, recording, or otherwise) without prior explicit written permission from the author for each use case.

For questions about acceptable use or bulk orders for schools, libraries, and institutions, please e-mail the author at donald@donaldjacobsen.com.

This is a work of fiction. All names, characters, businesses, places, events and incidents are fictitious. Any resemblance to real persons, entities, or events is purely coincidental.

ISBN (paperback) 978-1-7328273-6-3

BISAC Subjects:
1. JUV006000 JUVENILE FICTION / Business, Careers, Occupations
2. JUV071000 JUVENILE FICTION / Superheroes

This book belongs to:

Hi, My name is Hazel!
Can I tell you something cool?

My daddy is a NURSE
at a hospital!

Every day before he runs
off to work in a whirl,

he gives me a hug and says,
"I love you, sweet girl!"

I think that my dad being a nurse is so cool.

I tell all my friends about him at school!

My daddy talks to patients
to find out what's wrong.

He helps patients feel better
all day long!

When people get hurt,
daddy fixes their cuts.

To help them get healthy,
he sometimes gives shots.

My daddy checks out
how his patients are breathing

and listens to hear
how fast their heart's beating!

To check a blood pressure,
he inflates an arm cuff.

It gets really tight
when it gets pumped up!

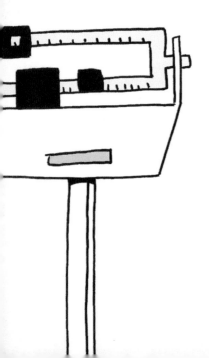

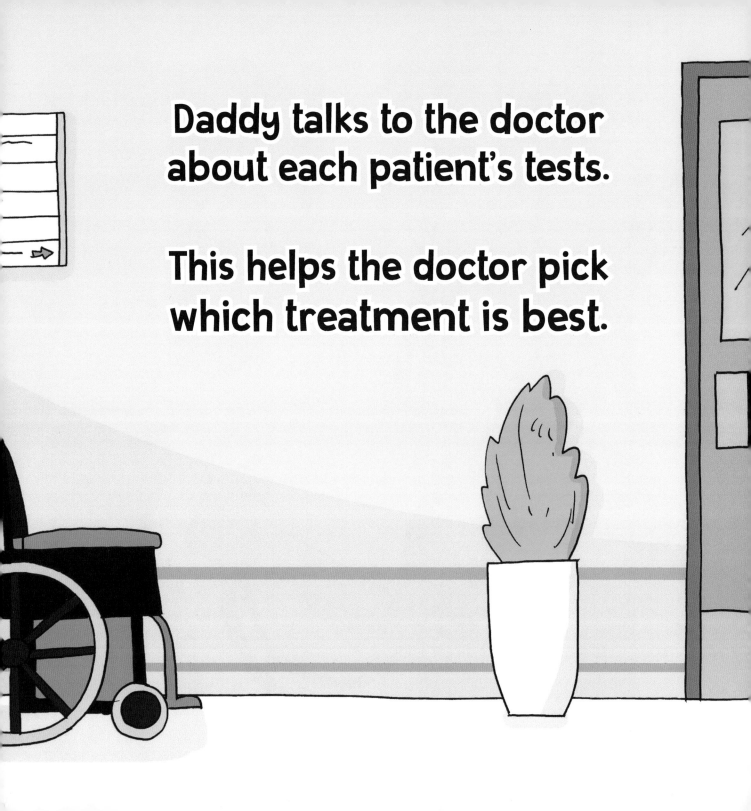

Daddy talks to the doctor about each patient's tests.

This helps the doctor pick which treatment is best.

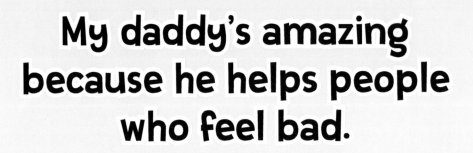

My daddy's amazing
because he helps people
who feel bad.

He's smart and he's strong
and that makes me so glad!

Late at night when my daddy comes home so tired, I run up to him with my arms open wide.

He picks me up and gives me a hug. I feel happy in his arms - so snug!

FREE audiobooks, coloring pages, and more!

Because you play such a challenging and meaningful role in the development of children, this book includes free audiobooks and other resources.

Go to the link below to get access to your free bonuses!

www.donaldjacobsen.com/freebies

If you loved this book, please leave a review on Amazon. Reviews are the best thank-you that you can give an author!

About the Author

Donald Jacobsen is a dad, husband, registered nurse, and sometimes-writer living and working in Memphis, Tennessee. When not busy working on his next book, he enjoys spending time with his wife, two daughters, and their mopey rescue dog, Yoda.

Learn more at www.donaldjacobsen.com.

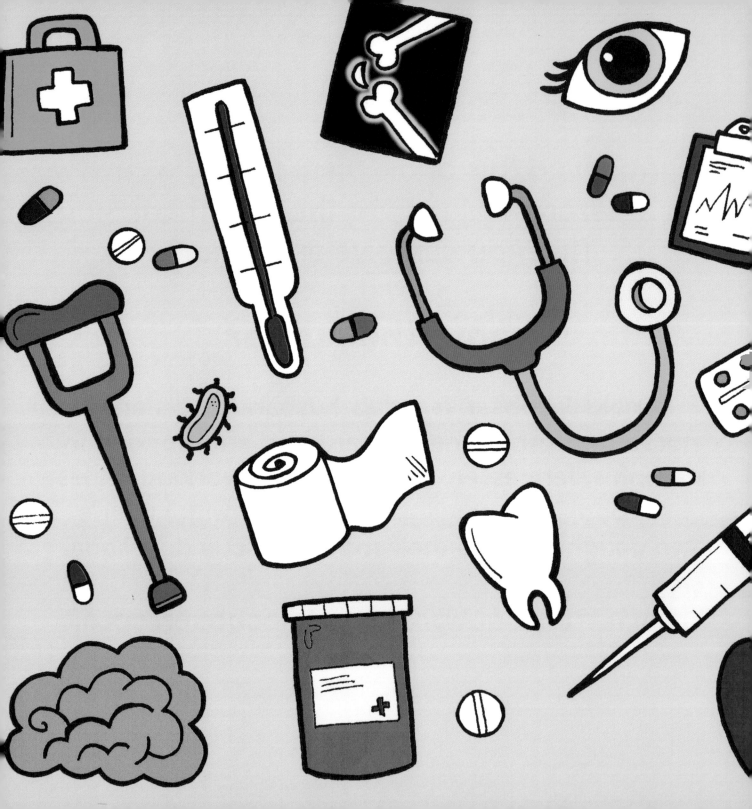

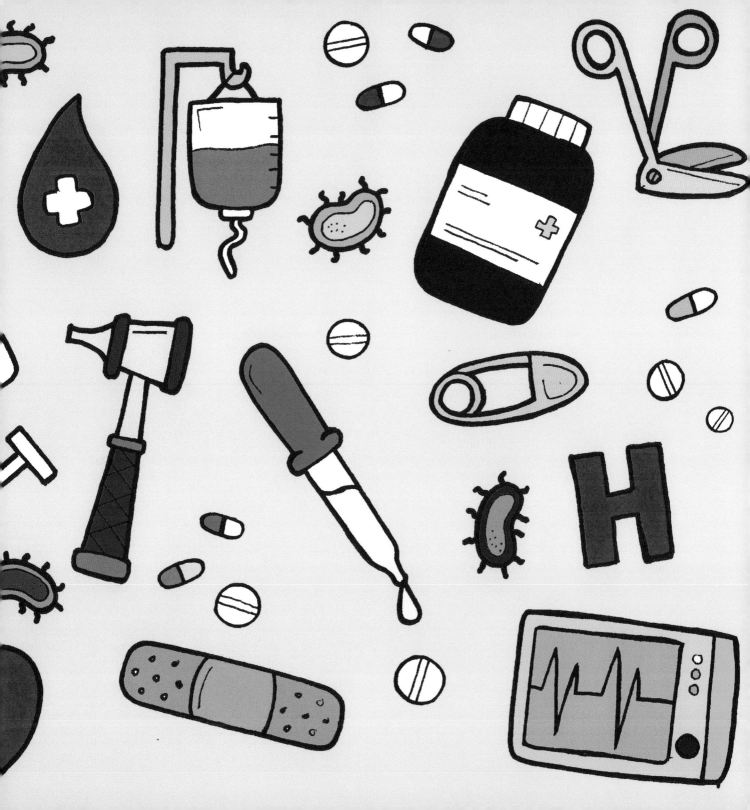

Printed in Great Britain
by Amazon

61306057R00017